FIVE HEAVENLY EMPERORS

After Pangu separated earth and sky, earth spirits moved up to the sky and became the first gods. They divided the universe into empires and elements. Each created his own empire and each controlled one of the five elements: earth, fire, wood, gold and water.

The Central Emperor was Xuan Yuan, and when he spoke everyone listened. He had four faces and could see in all directions. Because he was the emperor of the yellow earth he was known as the Yellow Emperor. The Earth Spirit was his servant and the Yellow Dragon guarded his heavenly court.

The Southern Emperor was the older brother of the Yellow Emperor. He controlled fire and summer and was known as the Blazing Emperor or Red Emperor. The Spirit of Fire was his servant and the Fire Bird guarded his heavenly court. The Chinese people consider themselves the descendants of the Yellow and Red Emperors.

The Eastern Emperor was Fushi. He controlled spring and was known as the Blue Emperor. The Spirit of Wood was his servant while the Blue Dragon guarded his heavenly court.

The Western Emperor was Shao Hao. He controlled autumn and was known as the White Emperor. The Spirit of Gold was his servant and his heavenly court was guarded by the White Tiger.

The Emperor of the North was Zhaun Xu. He controlled winter. As the sky in the north was always in darkness Zhaun Xu was also know as the Black Emperor. The Water Spirit was his servant and a creature that was half turtle and half snake guarded his heavenly court.

SONG NAN ZHANG

Five Heavenly Emperors

CHINESE MYTHS OF CREATION

TUNDRA BOOKS

PANGU SEPARATES
SKY AND EARTH

n the beginning the universe was a cloud of mist in the shape of a giant egg. Within it two creative forces emerged, the male, called *Yang,* and the female, called *Yin.*

From the union of the two, Pangu was born. As he stretched his arms and legs, the shell on the egg broke and the cloud separated. *Yang,* the light warm male matter, moved upward to form the sky and *Yin,* the heavier colder female matter, moved down to form the earth.

Pangu stood between them. As he grew over thousands of years, his head pushed up the sky and his feet pushed down the earth until he felt they were the right distance from each other.

His work finished, Pangu died and his body changed. His arms and legs became mountains holding earth and sky in place. His left eye became the sun and his right one the moon. The hair on his head became stars. His voice became thunder and lightning.

His skeleton became the five rivers of China. His blood became the water in those rivers and in the lakes and oceans, his veins the roadways and paths. His skin became the soil of the earth and the hairs on it became grass, flowers and trees. His teeth turned into diamonds. His breath became the cooling wind and the clouds that give rain.

Pangu became the universe we know. He had made the earth ready for people. But who would create them and who would teach them how to live? and a daughter.

2

On the rare occasions when the heavenly emperors visited earth they lived on Kunlun Mountain, a magical place of exotic creatures and plants. A monster with nine heads called Enlightenment guarded the mountaintop. On this magical mountain lived a six-headed woodpecker, many serpents and dragons, and the Fuchang tree that bore delicious fruit. The tree belonged to a phoenix who became very angry when he could not have his cherished fruit. It was guarded by a man with three heads that took turns sleeping so that he could always be on the watch for thieves.

On another part of the mountain was a tree that grew meat. Each piece of meat had an eye and was the best-tasting food in the world. The tree never got smaller because every time some meat was taken, a new piece would take its place.

The heavenly emperors had other gods – their relatives and guardians visited earth often and these gods stayed in the houses on Kunlun Mountain. It was these gods that would create humankind and teach it how to live.

NUWA MAKES HUMAN BEINGS

he gods were alone in the sky for a long time until one day they felt the need to create an intelligent being on earth that would entertain them and make the earth a lively place.

Fushi, the Eastern Emperor, had a younger sister called Nuwa. She often came down to earth to look for interesting things to do.

On one such visit, while resting on a hill, she picked up a handful of yellow clay and rolled it around in her hand. Pleased with how easy it was to shape, she tried molding a little statue to look like some of the gods she knew in heaven. When she was finished, she put it down beside her and, to her astonishment, it came to life.

Delighted with her creation, she made more and more little statues. As they danced around her, she said: "I'm going to call you 'human beings.'" She went on making them faster and faster until she was exhausted.

There seemed so many of them, but when she counted them there were only a few hundred. "Not enough," she decided. She mixed water with the clay and splashed it around. Every drop came alive. The hill of clay turned into tens of thousands of human beings.

She rushed back to heaven to tell the other gods about the creatures she had created in their image.

Ever since then human beings have ruled the earth. Those Nuwa sculpted by hand became the leaders; the others became followers.

Youchao and the First Dwellings

From the time they were created, people loved daylight for they could hunt and forage for food and see any danger ahead. But they were frightened at night.

In the dark, strange noises disturbed their sleep and wild beasts sometimes came out of the forest to attack them. Caves offered refuge, but these were so cold in winter some people froze, and so damp the rest of the year they were often sick.

One god did not like seeing people suffer. He came down to earth to see what he could do. One day as he sat under a tree wondering how he could help, he looked up and saw birds building a nest. Why don't I, he thought, teach people how to build nests for themselves?

The birds used a tree branch to hold their nest steady, so he used wood for a frame to hold up his dwelling. The birds used dry grass to weave their nest; he covered his frame with hay.

He liked the result so he taught people how to build shelters where they could be safe, warm and comfortable.

The people were so happy in their new homes, they honored the god by calling him Youchao, which means "Having Nest."

SHENNONG SHOWS HOW TO GROW FOOD

Gods never suffer from hunger, but human beings must spend most of their time searching for food. Animals and fish were easy to find in summer, but difficult in winter and many people died of starvation.

The Southern Emperor decided to help. It would be easier if people could live off plants which they could raise near their homes and store for the winter. He could teach them how to cultivate plants, but there was a more serious problem.

Among the millions of plants, which were safe to eat and which were poisonous?

The Southern Emperor set out on a tour of the earth, determined to taste every plant and make a list of those that were good to eat. It was slow work, so he invented a magic whip to help him. The whip could tell the qualities of a plant just by touching it. He also brought grains down from heaven and taught people how to plough, sow and harvest.

People honored the Southern Emperor by calling him Shennong, or the Peasant God.

The Central Emperor was so moved by what the Southern Emperor had done that he added a gift of his own, the nine-tassled golden wheat. It would result in many golden harvests and provide food that could be stored through the winter.

SUIREN MAKES FIRE

To the early humans, fire was dangerous and fascinating. When lightning set fire to dry wood in the forest, it was terrifying. Animals and people who could not run from it died. But when fire burned itself out, people found the ashes warmed them and roasted food. They saw that fire could be useful.

If only they could start a fire when they wanted to and control it.

Near the edge of the earth was a place that neither sunshine nor moonlight could reach. The only light came from a giant tree that sent out sparkles.

One day a traveling god walked by the tree and sat down to sleep. He was awakened by the sound of a nighthawk pecking at a branch above him. Every time the bird pecked, sparks came from the tree, dropped to the ground, and set fire to any dry leaves they touched.

If human beings had bits of the tree, the god realized, they could make fire whenever and wherever they wanted. He cut branches from it and taught people to drill on the dry wood and make sparks to start a fire.

The tree was called Flint because of the sparks it gave out, and the people, in gratitude to the god, called him Suiren, or Mr. Flint.

THE COWHERD AND THE WEAVING GIRL

Heaven and earth were not yet completely separated. In one place only the Heavenly River divided them and there human beings could approach the home of the gods.

The Yellow Emperor had many granddaughters. The Weaving Girl was the youngest. She lived on the eastern side of the Heavenly River and spent her days weaving cloth for the gods. When she needed a rest, she bathed in the river, singing beautiful songs.

One day a poor cowherd with his old water buffalo came to rest on the western side of the river. He heard the Weaving Girl singing and although he could not see her, he thought: "Whoever can sing like that must be very beautiful." He returned to the river every day to listen. "How can I get her attention?" he wondered. "I am only a cowherd. She will never look at me!"

The old water buffalo took pity on his master. "Cross the river," he said. "When she goes to bathe, hide her clothes. That will get her attention."

The Cowherd followed the advice and hid the Weaving Girl's clothes. He watched from behind a bush, saw that she was indeed as beautiful as her voice, and fell in love with her. When the Weaving Girl came ashore and found her clothes had been stolen, she was furious.

The Cowherd felt ashamed. He stood up and held out her clothes. "I'm sorry," he said. "I love you, but I am a poor cowherd with nothing to offer. Please forgive me." He bowed his head and turned to leave.

The Weaving Girl realized he was an honest and caring man. "Wait," she cried. "It's been so long since I've had anyone to talk to."

The Cowherd returned every day to speak with the Weaving Girl and she came to love him as well. She decided to give up her home in heaven and join him on the earth side of the river. They married and had a son and a daughter.

The Yellow Emperor was angered with his granddaughter's marriage to a mortal. He sent the Queen Mother and guardians to kidnap the Weaving Girl and bring her back to the Heavenly Empire. The Cowherd watched helplessly as his wife was taken from him and his children cried for their mother.

The old water buffalo again felt sorry for the Cowherd. "I am dying," he said. "Take my skin and fly on it to find your wife."

The Cowherd and his children used the skin to fly upward. But when the Queen Mother saw them approaching, she said: "How dare these mortals approach the Empire of the Gods!"

She took out her golden hairpin and drew a line in the sky between the gods and the Cowherd. The line became the Milky Way and was intended to divide heaven and earth and separate the Cowherd family forever.

The father and the children watched longingly from one side while the mother yearned for her husband and children from the other.

The Yellow Emperor was moved to pity by their grief. He decreed that his granddaughter could be with her husband and children once a year. On that day all the magpies on earth would go up to the sky and form a magic bridge which the Cowherd family could cross.

On a clear night you can see the Cowherd and the Weaving Girl as two bright stars on opposite sides of the Milky Way. But on one night each summer, if you look up at the sky, the two stars appear closer to each other. And when you see bald-headed magpies, you know they have no hair because the Cowherd family walks on top of their heads to be together.

FUSHI EXPLAINS
THE UNIVERSE

Fushi, the Eastern Emperor, did a lot to help people. He taught them how to make strings for their bows so they could hunt and how to knit nets so they could fish. He even invented a musical instrument, a pipe made of bamboo, so they would have entertainment.

He was very ambitious. He wanted to understand and explain the laws that ruled the universe. That would be the greatest gift he could give humankind.

For years he meditated. Every morning he sat upon his altar, listened to the tiniest sound coming from the earth and thought about it. Finally, he decided he had found the secret of existence.

He drew up a map to explain it. The circle in the center resembling an egg is Taichi, the beginning of the universe. The black and white halves, or *Yin* and *Yang*, stand for the female and male forces that control human existence. They join head to tail like a pair of fish. All life, every human being, has both *Yin* and *Yang* within. Happiness depends on their being in perfect balance.

The eight symbols around the Taichi are called Ba Gua. Each is a different combination of long lines, the *Yang*, and short lines, the *Yin*. Each symbol stands for one part of the laws that control the universe, telling us what has happened in history and what will happen in the future.

Fushi's map remains to this day a mystery, fascinating and challenging to mathematicians, scientists, and philosophers around the world.

Nuwu Mends the Sky

The earth was a peaceful place. Human beings were in harmony with each other and learning to do many things better.

But one day a terrible disaster struck. The dome-shaped sky split open and an endless rain poured down, flooding the earth. People and animals were swept away. A few survivors managed to get to the mountaintops, but there they were threatened by volcanoes erupting and hungry animals desperate for food.

The goddess Nuwa was horrified as she saw the people she had created being destroyed. She went to work to mend the sky.

She collected many five-colored stones and, using fire from heaven, she melted them down into hot lava. This she used to mend the cracks in the sky. She then sacrificed the great heavenly tortoise and used its legs to hold up the four corners of the sky.

When the sky was mended, she stopped the floods by creating lakes and dams out of ashes and earth.

At last the disaster was over, the earth was safe and all living things were at peace. Even the animals, birds, and snakes no longer used their teeth, claws or stings to hurt, but lived off plants.

Nuwa rode her winged dragon back to her heavenly home. She told the Yellow Emperor she wanted no honors for saving human life on earth, asked him to look after people in the future, and disappeared.

The inhabitants of earth never saw her again, but they ignored her request not to be honored and built giant statues and magnificent temples in her name.

YI SHOOTS DOWN NINE SUNS

n the outer edge of the Great Eastern Sea grew a tree of the gods called Fusan.

The god Dijun and his wife lived in a house built on top of the tree. She gave birth to ten suns that took turns climbing to the sky to warm and give light to the earth.

While one sun shone down from the heavens the other nine would bathe. They gave off so much heat that the water boiled around them like a pot of steaming soup, and the place came to be called Tanggu or "the soup basin."

Only the tree where they lived could withstand the heat. It had two trunks side by side and watched to make sure the brothers took turns rising and setting, so that only one sun would be in the sky at a time.

One day the ten suns felts mischievous. They all left the tree and rose into the sky at once. The earth suddenly became too hot for life. Crops withered. Forests caught fire. Rivers and lakes dried up. Animals that had been peaceful turned on each other before dying. The people thought they too would all die.

Yi was Dijun's guardian and he was very popular among the people. Yi was caught in a dilemma. He knew the suns were the children of his lord, but he had to save the earth. He took the red bow and white arrows that Dijun had given him many years ago and aimed them at the sky. One by one he shot down nine of the ten suns and left only one to give the right amount of light and heat to the earth.

Dijun never forgave Yi and barred him from returning to the sky.

Chang-Er Flies
to the Moon

Yi was pleased that he had saved the earth from too much heat and he liked living with people except, for one thing. He was troubled by the thought that one day he would die, like all human beings.

He went to the Queen of the West who lived on top of Jade Mountain to ask for help. She was the goddess in charge of magic medicines and she liked Yi for having saved life on earth. She reached into her robe and gave him a small pouch. "Keep this elixir in a safe place," she said. "At your dying moment, drink it and you will rise up to heaven."

Yi hid the elixir in his house and told no one except his wife, Chang-Er. She was curious as to what it might be like to fly and she often thought about the hidden elixir. One day she met a fortune-teller who said: "Tonight at sunset you will leave this world and end up in a place where you will be happy forever."

The fortune could have only one meaning. Chang-Er returned home and drank the elixir. Immediately her body became light as a feather and she felt herself fly upward toward the Moon Palace. But as soon as she entered it, she was turned into a toad. There she remains to this day and you can see her looking out when the moon is full.

Yi died of disappointment over his wife's betrayal. The Yellow Emperor felt Yi had been unfairly punished. He took him back to the heavenly empire and put him in charge of guarding it against demons and evil spirits.

THE BIRTH OF THE ALPHABET

While the Emperor Fushi was working out his laws of the universe, a minor god called Cangjie came up with an important invention. He was in charge of historical records. He kept an account of everything that happened by tying thousands of knots on thousands of ropes every day. He had two extra eyes to help but the work was still slow. He decided there must be a better way to keep records than using ropes.

One day, weary of work, he went for a walk. As he looked down at the ground in front of him, he saw a trail of animal footprints and got an idea. If people could look at footprints and know which animal had made them, why could they not look at picture-signs and know what they stood for?

He began to make simple drawings of everything he saw around him. He made thousands of sketches and made sure the people understood them. This was the beginning of the Chinese alphabet. Now they would be able to write letters to people far away, record history, and pass stories on to future generations.

As the years passed Cangjie's drawings became simpler and easier to copy. Although to this day many of the Chinese characters resemble the original drawings, most have to be learned one by one. It's hard work for Chinese children learning to read, but it means that people of the many different languages used throughout China can all understand what is written.

WHY GODS AND PEOPLE WERE FINALLY SEPARATED

For a long time gods and human beings lived in harmony. Gods me down to earth often to help people, and people could speak to the gods.

All this changed during the reign of Zhuan Xu, the great grandson of the Yellow Emperor. He was conceived when a brilliant light came toward his mother from the seventh star of the Plough, and he was born to rule many empires. At twelve he became Emperor of the West; at twenty he was enthroned as the Northern Emperor.

Soon after that a war broke out between the gods. They used men to fight in their armies in heaven and made men fight each other on earth.

When Zhuan Xu became Central Emperor in his old age, he decided there was only one way to stop the fighting. He sent his two most powerful grandsons, Zhong and Li, to destroy all the roads to heaven.

Zhong lifted the sky higher and Li pushed the earth further down. Zhong was assigned to keep peace in heaven and Li on earth.

Only one path was left between the two worlds. It was in the west across the Mountain of the Sun and Moon. Emperor Shuan Xu sent a giant god called Yei to guard the heavenly gate on top of the mountain. Yei has no arms but he can lift his two legs above his head to control the movements of the sun, moon and stars.

Yei rarely lets gods or humans pass the gate to interfere in each other's worlds.

I would like to give my best regards to Mr. Yuan Ke, who devoted his life to the study of Chinese mythology.

向畢生致力於中國古代神話研究的袁珂先生致敬意

Original edition published by Tundra Books, Montreal, 1994
This edition published by Tundra Books, Toronto, 2002
Copyright © 1994, 2002 by Song Nan Zhang
With additional translations from Chinese to English by Hao Yu Zhang

Published in Canada by Tundra Books,
481 University Avenue, Toronto, Ontario M5G 2E9

Published in the United States by Tundra Books of Northern New York,
P.O. Box 1030, Plattsburgh, New York 12901

Library of Congress Control Number: 93-61794

National Library of Canada Cataloguing in Publication Data

Zhang, Song Nan, 1942-
    Five heavenly emperors : Chinese myths of creation / Song Nan Zhang.

ISBN 0-88776-338-3

1. Chinese – Folklore – Juvenile literature. 2. Creation – Folklore – Juvenile literature. I. Title.

BL1802.Z43 1994   j398.2'089'951   C94-900052-3 rev

We acknowledge the support of the Canada Council for the Arts and the Ontario Arts Council for our publishing program.

We acknowledge the financial support of the Government of Canada through the Book Publishing Industry Development Program for our publishing activities.

Design: Blaine Herrmann

Printed in Hong Kong, China

2 3 4 5 6   06 05 04 03 02